Winnie-the-Pooh
Pooh Invents a New Game

Adapted from the stories by A.A. Milne

One day, as Pooh was walking towards the wooden bridge which crosses the river, he was trying to make up a piece of poetry about fir-cones, because there they were, lying about on each side of him, and he felt singy.

So he picked a fir-cone up, and looked at it, and said to himself, "This is a very good fir-cone, and something ought to be done with it."
But he couldn't think of anything.

And then this came into his head suddenly:

Here is a myst'ry
About a little fir-tree.
Owl says it's his tree,
And Kanga says it's her tree.

"Which doesn't make sense," said Pooh, "because Kanga doesn't live in a tree."

He had just come to the bridge; and not looking where he was going, he tripped over something, and the fir-cone jerked out of his paw into the river.

"Bother," said Pooh, as it floated slowly under the bridge, and he went back to get another fir-cone which had a rhyme to it. But then he thought that he would just look at the river instead, because it was a peaceful sort of day, so he lay down and looked at it, and it slipped slowly away beneath him . . . and suddenly, there was his fir-cone slipping away too.

"That's funny," said Pooh. "I dropped it on the other side," said Pooh, "and it came out on this side! I wonder if it would do it again?" And he went back for some more fir-cones.

It did. It kept on doing it. Then he dropped two in
at once, and leant over the bridge to see which of them
would come out first; and one of them did; but as they
were both the same size, he didn't know if it was the
one which he wanted to win, or the other one.

And that was the beginning
of the game called Poohsticks,
which Pooh invented, and
which he and his friends used
to play on the edge of the Forest.
But they played with sticks instead of fir-cones, because
they were easier to mark.

Now one day Pooh and Piglet and Rabbit and Roo
were all playing Poohsticks together. They had dropped
their sticks in when Rabbit said "Go!" and then they
had hurried across to the other side of the bridge, and
now they were all leaning over the edge, waiting to see
whose stick would come out first.

"I can see mine!" cried Roo. "No, I can't, it's
something else. Can you see yours, Piglet? I thought
I could see mine, but I couldn't. There it is! No, it isn't.
Can you see yours, Pooh?"

"No," said Pooh.

"Mine's a sort of greyish one," said Piglet, not daring
to lean too far over in case he fell in.

"Yes, that's what I can see. It's coming over on
to my side."

Rabbit leant over further than ever, looking for his,
and Roo wriggled up and down, calling out "Come on,
stick! Stick, stick, stick!" and Piglet got very excited
because his was the only one which had been seen, and
that meant that he was winning.

"It's coming!" said Pooh.
"Are you sure it's mine?" squeaked Piglet excitedly.
"Yes, because it's grey. A big grey one. Here it comes!
A very – big – grey – Oh, no, it isn't, it's Eeyore."
And out floated Eeyore.
"Eeyore!" cried everybody.

Looking very calm, very dignified, with his legs
in the air, came Eeyore from beneath the bridge.

"It's Eeyore!" cried Roo, terribly excited.

"Is that so?" said Eeyore, getting caught up by
a little eddy, and turning slowly round three times.
"I wondered."

"I didn't know you were playing," said Roo.

"I'm not," said Eeyore.

"Eeyore, what are you doing there?" said Rabbit.

"I'll give you three guesses, Rabbit. Digging holes in the ground? Wrong. Leaping from branch to branch of a young oak-tree? Wrong. Waiting for somebody to help me out of the river? Right. Give Rabbit time, and he'll always get the answer."

"But Eeyore," said Pooh in distress, "what can we – I mean, how shall we – do you think if we –"

"Yes," said Eeyore. "One of those would be just the thing. Thank you, Pooh."

There was a moment's silence while everybody thought.

"I've got a sort of idea," said Pooh at last, "but I don't suppose it's a very good one."

"I don't suppose it is either," said Eeyore.

"Go on, Pooh," said Rabbit. "Let's have it."

"Well, if we all threw stones and things into the river on one side of Eeyore, the stones would make waves, and the waves would wash him to the other side."

"That's a very good idea," said Rabbit, and Pooh looked happy again.

"Very," said Eeyore. "When I want to be washed, Pooh, I'll let you know."

But Pooh had got the biggest stone he could carry, and was leaning over the bridge, holding it in his paws.

"I'm not throwing it, I'm dropping it, Eeyore," he explained. "And then I can't miss – I mean I can't hit you. Could you stop turning round for a moment, because it muddles me rather?"

"No," said Eeyore. "I like turning round."

Pooh dropped his stone. There was a loud splash, and Eeyore disappeared . . .

And then, just as Pooh was beginning to think
that he must have chosen the wrong day for his Idea,
something grey showed for a moment by the river
bank . . . and it got slowly bigger and bigger . . . and at
last it was Eeyore coming out.

With a shout they rushed off the bridge, and pushed
and pulled at him; and soon he was standing among
them again on dry land.
"Oh, Eeyore, you are wet!" said Piglet,
feeling him.

Eeyore shook himself, and asked somebody to explain to Piglet what happened when you had been inside a river for quite a long time.

"How did you fall in, Eeyore?" asked Rabbit, as he dried him with Piglet's handkerchief.

"I was BOUNCED," said Eeyore.

"Oo," said Roo excitedly, "did somebody push you?"

"Somebody BOUNCED me. I was just thinking by the side of the river – thinking, if any of you know what that means – when I received a loud BOUNCE."

"Oh, Eeyore!" said everybody.

"But who did it?" asked Roo.

Eeyore didn't answer.

"I expect it was Tigger," said Piglet nervously.

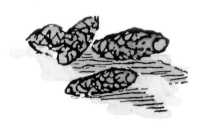

"But, Eeyore," said Pooh, "was it a Joke, or an Accident? I mean –"

"I didn't stop to ask, Pooh. Even at the very bottom of the river I didn't stop to say to myself, 'Is this a Hearty Joke, or is it the Merest Accident?' I just floated to the surface, and said to myself, 'It's wet.' If you know what I mean."

"And where was Tigger?" asked Rabbit.

Before Eeyore could answer, there was a loud noise behind them, and through the hedge came Tigger himself.

"Hallo, everybody," said Tigger cheerfully.

"Hallo, Tigger," said Roo.

Rabbit became very important suddenly.

"Tigger," he said solemnly, "what happened just now?"

"Just when?" said Tigger a little uncomfortably.

"When you bounced Eeyore into the river."

"I didn't bounce him."

"You bounced me," said Eeyore gruffly.

"I didn't really. I had a cough, and I happened to be behind Eeyore, and I said 'Grr-oppp-ptschschschz'."

"That's what I call bouncing," said Eeyore. "Taking people by surprise. Very unpleasant habit."

"I didn't bounce, I coughed," said Tigger crossly.

"Bouncy or Coffy, it's all the same at the bottom of the river."

"Well," said Rabbit, "all I can say is – well, here's Christopher Robin, so he can say it."

Christopher Robin came down from the Forest to the bridge, feeling all sunny and careless, and just as if twice nineteen didn't matter a bit, as it didn't on such a happy afternoon.

"It's like this, Christopher Robin," began
Rabbit, "Tigger –"

"All I did was I coughed," said Tigger.

"He bounced," said Eeyore.

"Well, I sort of boffed," said Tigger.

"Hush!" said Rabbit, holding up his paw.
"What does Christopher Robin think about it
all? That's the point."

"Well," said Christopher Robin, not quite sure
what it was all about. "I think –"

"Yes?" said everybody.

"I think we all ought to play Poohsticks."

So they did. And Eeyore, who had never played it before, won more times than anybody else; and Roo fell in twice, the first time by accident and the second time on purpose, because he suddenly saw Kanga coming from the Forest, and he knew he'd have to go to bed anyhow.

So then Rabbit said he'd go with them; and Tigger
and Eeyore went off together, because Eeyore wanted
to tell Tigger How to Win at Poohsticks; and
Christopher Robin and Pooh and Piglet were left
on the bridge by themselves.

For a long time they looked at the river beneath them, saying nothing, and the river said nothing too, for it felt very quiet and peaceful on this summer afternoon.

"Tigger is all right, really," said Piglet lazily.

"Of course he is," said Christopher Robin.

"Everybody is really," said Pooh. "That's what I think," said Pooh. "But I don't suppose I'm right," he said.

"Of course you are," said Christopher Robin.

First published in this edition in 2001 by Methuen Children's Books, an imprint of
Egmont Children's Books Limited, a division of Egmont Holding Limited
239 Kensington High Street, London W8 6SA

Printed in China
ISBN 0 416 19969 0